Sinchi

GIUSEPPE BARTOLI

Edited with additional notes by
Oliver Jones

 EYEWEAR PUBLISHING

SINCHI

Sinchi is Quechua for warrior. During the period of the Peruvian Internal Conflict the government deployed the *Sinchis* (an American-funded counterterrorist brigade) to combat *Sendero Luminoso*. They were notorious for human rights violations.

First published in 2017
by Eyewear Publishing Ltd
Suite 333, 19-21 Crawford Street
Marylebone, London w1h 1pj
United Kingdom

Cover design and typeset by Edwin Smet
Printed in England by TJ International Ltd, Padstow, Cornwall

isbn 978-1-911335-96-2

*Eyewear wishes to thank Jonathan Wonham for his
generous patronage of our press.*

This is a work of creative nonfiction; all of the persons depicted
in the novella are fictitious and in no way represent real individuals.

WWW.EYEWEARPUBLISHING.COM

Giuseppe Bartoli
is a Peruvian-Italian-American
writer, whose poetry and prose
is published widely, in the UK,
America, and Peru. He has lived in
the UK, Italy, France, and Spain,
as well as across South America.
This is his debut novel
in English.

•

Oliver Jones (editor)
is Peruvian-British, and has a BA
from Oxford. He is an editor
at Eyewear and the author
of several books.

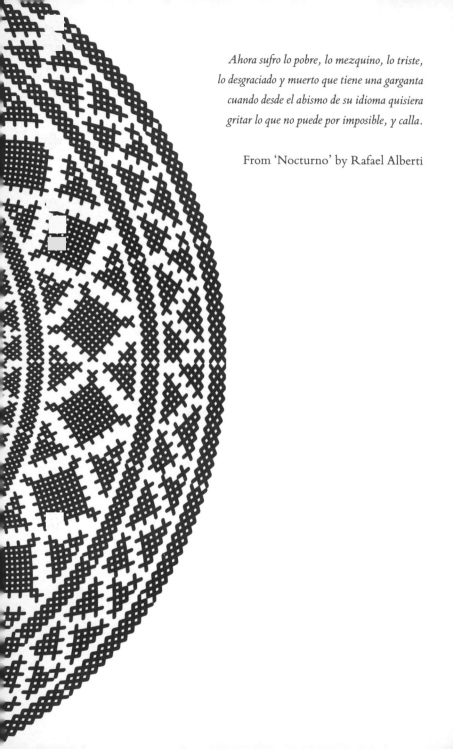

Ahora sufro lo pobre, lo mezquino, lo triste,
lo desgraciado y muerto que tiene una garganta
cuando desde el abismo de su idioma quisiera
gritar lo que no puede por imposible, y calla.

From 'Nocturno' by Rafael Alberti

The only thing more dreadful than the sight of shit is stepping on it. Even worse, being covered in it, like the character of Santiago Nasar in the opening aperçu of *Crónica de una Muerte Anunciada*. Llama. Guanaco. Vicuña, if you can afford it[1]. Specifics don't matter, because shit is shit. And being full of it is just as bad.

Speaking of shit, if it hadn't been for a hint of twilight, this place would appear to be the asshole of the world. Time-wise, it could go either way, as Inti could easily be confused with Mama Quillya[2]. That is why the Incas built temples for both. Just in case. For moments like this when a random deity might prove to be the difference between living and dying.

This also helps to explain why the Incas built so many of these temples around the empire – just to be safe – like their never-ending litany of gods. Illapa[3]. Pachamama[4]. Mama Cocha[5]. Pacha Kamaq. Pariacaca[6]. None worked out. None of them came to the Inca's rescue when they confused the Spanish for their intangible gods.

Maybe the Spanish were the best thing that ever happened to the Incas. Had they been monotheists, perhaps they'd still be around. Sometimes, what appears to be our salvation is in truth the source of our demise.

Refocusing on the sky, it looks like a giant ripe avocado split in half. However, both the pulp and pip of the new day are tightly fastened to the rind of yesterday. Clinging. Its dark texture resembles a pair of black special unit commando boots, imprinting their leathery darkness all over the heavens. And with each impression left behind, there's the possibility of the godless militant whose boots match the footprint.

Men. Women. Children. Treading. Stomping. Marching. Fighting. Dying. And as you read this, their strides begin to echo off your subconscious mind. Giving form. Features. Faces. Fingers. Taking shape and filling in the shades. It's not until you hear their voices – pleas, shouts, shrieks – that the nothingness produces in you the impression of nonbeing. The hysteria is interrupted by a series of guttural noises, similar to coughs, seeking an ear to become sound.

Disoriented by the blankness, finding the source of these noises is like being a bat stuck in infinite space: the sounds have nowhere to bounce off. Perspective is impossible. However, a sign of hope arrives with the passing of a few more minutes, as the sounds begin to travel at intervals, much like waves. It must be Mama Cocha's way of letting her sisters Pachamama and Pariacaca know about the coming dead and the disappeared.

Crashing waves. Crashed economy. Crash course. I cannot hear their voices, see their faces, as before. The spume is ash, and ash proverbially returns to dust. Covering books. Shelves. Hands. Homes. Everything is crushed into a finer powder with each subsequent car bomb. Spewing more dust into the air, until we breathe nothing but ourselves. Our generation will be remembered as air. Vanished. *Los desaparecidos*[7].

However, the ensuing darkness has no intention of disappearing, as it makes its presence felt, once again, transmitting a series of crunching sounds without revealing their source. Similar to sitting for over twenty hours on an interprovincial bus next to a *paisano* nibbling on *charqui* or *chacchando*[8] coca leaves with his mouth open, our eavesdropping pays dividends, as the exasperating munching noises make you forget all about the feelings of uncertainty triggered by the inescapable darkness.

Unfortunately, these unpleasant noises cannot prevent the mind from drawing an infinite number of absurd conclusions about the origins of these sounds. Of all peoples, Peruvians take this mannerism and turn it into an art, such is their ability to manipulate that fine line between fact and fiction. For example, when something doesn't sound or seem convenient, Peruvians cover their faces with a black mantilla, as if saying *to me this sounds just as good as the truth, so it must be fact*.

Copernicus! I'm sorry to tell you, but in this country you are wrong. Latin America is your antithesis. Here, the world's not heliocentric: it's Lima-centric. And in Lima, not knowing is worse than bluffing it. So how can you blame the gossip-mongering citizens of a tabloid-dependent nation for making assertions?

Here, a scandal sheet – which reads much like a magical realism novel – might set you back

50p, but a book could cost you up to a week's wages. Here, Monopoly's a game and not the reason there's only one newspaper left to cover a country six times the size of England. Here, self-importance and false prejudices are the unwritten laws of the land. Here, what is printed in capital letters revolves around the first city. Here, we have not even begun to scrape the surface of what's really wrong with Peru.

Like a heart heading into tachycardia – not rest, or arrest – the pair of black special unit commando boots that is the night, can be heard moving. Treading. Stomping. Marching. The brain cannot help itself anymore. It accelerates. The particles of thought are light. Travelling. Conclusions begin to draw themselves, as if saying *Deng Xiaoping, you son of a bitch*: I've been here all along! Warning of the true message behind the hanging hides. Wanting to cut off the nooses of guilt that have been tied on my mental lampposts since the 26th of December, 1980[9].

I've been waking up ever since in the middle of the night. Sweat-covered. Words on the tip of my tongue. Cangallo. Huamanga. Huanca Sancos. La Mar. Lucanas. Parinacochas. Paucar del Sara Sara. Sucre. Víctor Fajardo. Vilcas Huamán. Huanta[10]. It's not my fault they died first in my dreams, and then in real life. I might as well have been subconsciously a *terrorista*. An *MRtista*[11]. A *Senderista*[12].

Maybe I should have been the most insignificant columnist for the cheapest tabloid in the nation. Underpaid. Unnoticeable. Untraceable. Unprincipled. Willing to spread gossip all over the toast of truth. They pay for my lies because they cannot come up with their own. And gossip's just what the inner doctor prescribes – only 50p per dose per morning – to momentarily block out the insecurities of the time, even before you hit page three.

Power outages. Curfews. Food shortages. Coups d'état. Murders. Disappearances. Corruption. Terrorism. Given the quality of the press and education in this country: I think they might be watching too much *MacGyver*[13].

The real impossibility though, is not to think too much about things. Because the more you stop and think about them, during times of uncertainty neither work nor truth will set you free. So why protect either? Dying in the name of the truth won't maintain your family when you're gone. The state's not going to verify with the Real Academia Española if your version of the word 'honesty' matches theirs. Faith. Fact. Fulfilment. These are all dependent on your surroundings, and here there are no guarantees except the right to remain silent.

On the 26th of December, 1980, guarantees were hung from lampposts alongside dogs.

Now we are the hanging dogs, marking the death of a magical realism in which Peruvians have been living for too long. All we are left with is a reality where the heads of the terrorist organisations are highly educated scholars and the general population averages less than one book per person per year.

That is why I fear Peru might not survive: because our weaknesses play too well into the opposing forces' strengths. They've known it ever since the 26th of December, 1980, when the population was too unaware, too ignorant, and too detached from the world to be able to read between the lines. Hence, they know we have no bluff; they've already called it.

Even if we're lucky enough to win, I'm willing to bet that history books ten, fifteen, twenty years from now won't talk about what happened. *Desaparecidos*. Most won't remember that there ever was a war. In Peru, people tend to forget quickly. And re-elect. And release. And return right back to where they're starting from. Two steps forward and three steps back. *Más vale malo conocido que bueno por conocer*[14].

Anything can happen in this country. Who knows, maybe one day the future of the nation – adolescents, students, protesters, young parents – might wake up and decide that all the imprisoned terrorists are in fact political prisoners. The presidential band on the shoulders of the leader of their choice would be like the two-thirds Inca genetic majority surrendering once again to the Catholic invader, mistaken for a god.

I find myself blabbering again. But I guess that's to be expected since I too am a Peruvian. Though, I have a secret for you. Something most people don't know about me: I was born in the United States. That makes me a nationalised Peruvian, a legal alien, a true American. Because who's more Peruvian: the one who's born here or the one who chooses to be here?

And now the 'state of emergency' that is the surrounding darkness is partially lifted, as daylight creeps through the curtain nooks of night and into our wakening bloodshot eyes. And while our vision focuses, the question of *where we are* becomes the only suitable topic of discussion. A discussion that is partly resolved in the time it takes for an image to be inverted by the brain. The lack of cars, lights, sounds, motion, and people suggests that we're in the provinces.

Speaking of the provinces, if it hasn't been made clear yet: Lima is Peru. Another ten minutes pass and I get the feeling it must be so. Here, the number of roads appears to be limited. Here, the number of lampposts lighting those limited roads are even scarcer. Here, we are outside of the range of the capital's electrical pylons. Here there's nothing. Not even a human being, and that's the least worrying thing about it.

Even the Incas had a better perception as to where things were going. No asphalted roads. No computer models. No weather satellites. Yet, they still knew when to plant and when to harvest. That's because the true Inca gold was red, uncomplicated, and natural. It was *mullu* – or *spondylus* – a red mollusc found between the coasts of Ecuador and Peru. By finding too many or too few, the Incas could predict how much rain to expect. As for us, all we can predict is uncertainty.

A few minutes go by and unlike mankind, Pachamama and her siblings Illapa and Pariacaca decide to aid us by mercifully echoing into our blind ears a repetitive splatting sound. It seems that the Inca gods are trying to tell us something. Remind us of something. Connect us with something that has been lost. So we lend our ear and listen. The wet splattering sound is the sound made by army boots, treading knee-deep in mud.

The Inca gods' subtle hints tell us that we are not in Lima, because it never rains there. It only drizzles lightly from time to time. In other words, there's not enough moisture in the ground to form mud. Maybe that means that we're in the jungle. Then again, it couldn't be. Here, the silence is deafening. No animals. No waterfalls. No... the only region left for us to choose from is the Andes. Yes, that's where we are: somewhere deep in *la Cordillera de los Andes*[15]. A small, unmapped village. A village that in times of terrorism does not welcome foreigners for fear of further persecution. A village dangerously similar to Uchuraccay[16].

A further swell of sunbeams breaking onto the hillside seems to prove our hypothesis. We are in the Andes. Light begins to pencil in the outskirts of a house or two on the horizon. The greenness covered in morning dew acts like a prism, refracting the light back into our eyes. We are blind in the middle of nowhere. No clouds, no sunglasses. We are forced to wait until condensation crowns the mountaintops that rise like heads out of the mud, rock, and verdure to calm our disorientation.

At half the distance to the houses, a small lake formed out of natural springs, rain, and mudslides provides a traveller with an ideal resting spot. A few trees stand in the shade of their neighbour. Also, it offers a map as to where we are going: two houses are reflected in the water. This is Pachamama's GPS. Perhaps, we have accidentally arrived at Paykikin: the last city of the Incas.

However, a visual inventory reveals the work of *comuneros*[17], not that of Incas. The two slanted half-brick, half-adobe houses are in need of repair. As a side adornment, half a dozen sheared llama await us, walking in their own shit. What we thought were Inca ruins turn out to be an encircling stone wall on life-support, dividing the limits between the two houses and their miniscule pastures. Yet there's the feeling of being somewhere uninhabited, somewhere lost, as the vacancy of the night unsettles us. This is our *mullu,* our red mollusc.

The nothingness also reveals to us is that we have been in the presence of a human being all along. His silhouette gives him away, a shadow that appears to be heading towards the abandoned houses. A black blur that isn't fully visible. Our *mullu* tells us: blackness that heads into nothingness cannot be a good sign of things to come.

Although this person's features cannot be determined, some peculiarities surface. For example, with each step he makes, he grows more and more tired; or so we assume from how the silhouette pauses every couple of minutes. Not only are we in the Andes, but also we must be at least two-to-three thousand metres above sea level, judging by the pauses, which are becoming more and more frequent. This individual has either not bothered to acclimatise himself with the altitude, or he is from the coastal region. It's more than probable that he comes from Lima.

But Pachamama is in a playful mood today, and she whispers to Inti to press pause on the dawn. The unusual hiatus makes the blurred man seem like a character from a short movie, struggling to move up an incline as if in slow motion. As the minutes pass, the blur grows apelike, as the homo sapiens knuckles down to his primate instincts. Poster child for human evolution: the incline begins to show signs of flatness; the man grows erect until his silhouette resembles that of the familiar homo sapiens once again.

Treading knee-deep in mud and probably llama shit, by the smell of it, the man appears to be exhausted. He presses on like a *tren de sierra*[18], halting only a few metres shy of one of the half-stone, half-adobe houses. Using the crumbled stone wall as a chair, his backside fits in perfectly where a large stone has gone missing. Tired. Sweating. Coughing. He gasps for air like an asthmatic.

The houses are in a deplorable condition. The doors are chipped. There are man-sized holes on the roofs. Half the shutters are broken, the other half missing. Adobe bricks have been jammed into places where stones have gone missing. The floors are covered in dirt. Correction: the floors are dirt. The smell of manure comes from inside the houses. In short, it looks as if either an earthquake or a mudslide has struck the premises; especially the way a section of one of the houses has collapsed. The main support beam of the house is a mould-covered splinter, long as an arm. It looks like a finger pointing up to the heavens, as if crying *save me oh blessed father*.

Salvation is like location – it's a relative issue – and the more you study, the more you feel you will attain neither. The half-dozen llamas have been sheared, so they're not wild. Either someone lives here part of the time, or there must be a village nearby. Let us hope it's one of the two. Otherwise, the *comuneros* must have heard us coming and are hiding in fear. If that's the case, then it's time to worry. After all, the *comuneros* have been through an incredible ordeal at the hands of the military, paramilitary, and the terrorists. They can't trust anyone. And for that reason, we run the risk of being confused with *Senderistas*. We could end up like the seven journalists who were lynched at Uchuraccay. Or worse.

Though what can be worse than knowing that the ones who claim they are fighting for you are the ones who are threatening your very existence? The terrorists are supposedly fighting for better living conditions, while military and paramilitary groups seek to create stability and order. But neither are doing what they are supposed to be doing. Nobody is really fighting for the *comuneros*. The *comuneros* have become sacrificial pawns. Their deaths are used as a political tool by both sides. Only their deaths give them any power.

They have no DNIs[19]. No land titles. No proof of address. No bank accounts. No phones. Who would miss them? Who would bother to find out what happened to them? Technically, they don't exist. The census bureau does not have a special helicopter in order to discover them. It would cost the internal revenue service more money to collect than they'd ever get out of it. And that's assuming the *comuneros* use money and not *trueque*[20]. It's not until you take one good long look at them – square in the eyes – that you'll discover that all you can truly find in these small Andean communities are ghosts: thousands of Holy Ghosts forgotten by the Catholic Church.

How about a prayer for their souls? *In the name of the Father, the Son and the Holy* – ghosts are exactly what you'd expect to find, wherever it is we are, as the unidentifiable silhouette leaves the two half-stone, half-adobe deserted houses.

One more time, like a *tren de sierra*, slowly but surely, he ascends towards the top of the mountain. Perhaps, that's where we'll find the llama shearers. He starts. Stops. Restarts. Stops. Restarts again. Tiring. Slowing. Wobbling. Like a shaman praying for rain. Pariacaca nods, as if saying *not now*. Staggering. Trying to drag himself along, the bewitched shadow tries to dance through the pain. He assumes the apelike position once again. He grunts as if marking territory.

At the top of the mountain he arrives at a town, he meets a welcoming party composed of half a dozen anorexic, unenthusiastic llamas, a few pigs that smell more of llama shit than their own, and a small pit filled with guinea pigs one step away from the dinner plate. They greet the stranger with the traditional, provincial indifference. Or maybe the animals are reciprocating the indifference they sense in the individual? Whatever it is, I'm sure the mountain is not the only one in need of a bath.

No soap bar could wash away the awkward feeling of having ventured into the past. Each step further into this village feels like taking a step back in time. The War of the Pacific. Colonial rule. The Inca Empire. It feels as if we have become the enemy, first by trespassing, then by forcing our ways onto them. Thanks to terrorism, Robespierre's *let terror be the order of the day* became the law of the land. State of emergency. Curfews. Uprisings. Coups. Assassinations. Car bombs. Protests. The entire country is in turmoil and for some strange reason, being here now feels like a sign of solidarity with those who have been forgotten. There's no explanation for my mood swing – maybe it's the lack of oxygen that is starting to play games with my mind.

My sanity returns when the coca leaves of thought are chewed into reality by the light of day, which has rendered the man visible. I say man, and not woman, because of his facial features. Height. Attire. Location. The black fatigues. The woolly cap. The Outer Tactical Vest, M16 assault rifle and worn-down pair of black special unit commando boots.

Black fatigues can only mean one thing: he is a *Sinchi*[21]. Notorious for supposedly fighting the terrorists alongside the *ronderos* and *comuneros*, the *Sinchis* are an American counterterrorist brigade known for their brutality. Beatings. Rape. Disappearances. Mass graves. Murders. But don't bother trying to research it: you won't find that information in the papers. Books. Anywhere.

What was once a term of respect, honour, and duty in the Inca Empire — *sinchi* meaning a warrior — has now been reduced to the equivalent of a hired mercenary; a pillager. No God. No gold. No glory. The *Sinchis* are out to protect their own interests, Lima's, and most importantly the American government's. The latter comes as no surprise to Latin Americans.

American involvement or not, who's going to patrol the Andes and make sure the *Sinchis* are respecting human rights? The UN? NATO? Mercosur? Try no one. If they committed any crimes, it was with the hindsight of future immunity; especially since any crimes committed outside the range of Lima's electrical pylons are practically invisible.

That is, assuming its citizens are even looking.

Besides, you don't need both sides of a story to run an editorial. Just as long as the other side has no say in it. And that is probably why, after the events at Uchuraccay, the *comuneros* were branded as barbaric murderers. They had no radios. Televisions. Phones. Computers. Paper. Not even a written language. How could the *comuneros* defend themselves? No one cared if these 'barbaric murderers' were only acting on the advice of government agents. Or that they had endured a wave of attacks from *Senderistas*, military, and paramilitary forces. They were poorly armed, unskilled, and paranoid. To them, every visitor was a possible double agent.

Accidental or not, it doesn't matter. The whole country is a no man's land, especially Ayacucho[22]. It seems being the poorest region in the nation was not punishment enough, so *Sendero Luminoso* made it both its hub and place of social experiment; an experiment which in theory intended to turn Ayacucho into a collective.

However, the *Senderistas* overlooked two significant details: (1) the word *commune* – or *comuna* – is already found within the turn of phrase *comuneros*, and (2) the *comuneros* had little or nothing to share at all. But that was to be expected, given that Ayacucho was Quechua for *death's corner*. It's almost as if the name itself calls upon Pariacaca to meet its predetermined future. Ayacucho is the Peruvian Manifest Destiny.

But none of these are the reason why the *comuneros* and *ronderos* stay out of the *Sinchis'* way. *Sinchis* are better armed. Trained. Uniformed. Supplied. Plus, the *comuneros* and *ronderos* travel by foot whereas the *Sinchis* use helicopters. And that's how the locals were taught to stay alert: if they don't come by helicopter, then they're not *Sinchis*. Everyone else is live target practice.

Driving range. Long range. No range. I wonder what rank he is? It is probably best not to enquire as to the nature of his visit. What is it? Just look away, so as not to arouse suspicion. Calm. Collected. Cool. Let everyone know you're there, but not. Make yourself one of the living *desaparecidos*. With the *Sinchis*, everything is unpredictable. So take a swig. Have a smoke. Actually, don't do either. They might want some or … the more I think about it, the more I realise that there's really no successful way of dealing with the possibility of death. This lesson comes from a childhood of being surrounded constantly by such an excess of violence that its absence instils you with the greatest sense of fear and insecurity of all.

Confidently, the man places a filter into one of the ends of a roll-up paper. He folds it into the shape of a cigarette by licking it along the wide end, dropping a fine mist of dried-up tobacco on the ground as he does so. You'd think he was giving thanks to Pachamama.

Before lighting it, he pauses to put a browned envelope filled with tobacco into one of the breast pockets of his Outer Tactical Vest, along with an old cardboard pack of Marlboros he's using to assemble his filters and the half-empty, green packet of French rolling paper. He reaches into an adjacent pocket to pull out a gold Zippo lighter with a *Tumi* engraved on the knuckle side. In one suave motion, the lighter opens, the wicket lights and with the other hand covering the flame from the wind, the man bends his head downwards to consecrate his homemade cigarette. After a few initial puffs, he breaks into a circular stride, almost as if performing a native ritual dance.

The offering has been made and the sacrament received. But what stands out the most, what shouldn't go unnoticed, what's most troubling, is the fact that the man decided not to throw his cigarette stub on the ground. This is most un-Peruvian. If this were Lima that stub would hit the ground quicker than you can blink, even if there's a municipal trashcan only metres away. Throwing garbage on the ground is a national pastime. Jaywalking is a national sport. The car horn is a national instrument. Tabloids are a national quest for knowledge. His disregard for these *tradiciones Peruanas* tells us that he is either a foreigner or highly educated. Or both.

Let us hope it is both. That way he'll have the common sense to get the hell out of here while the going is good. But how smart can he really be if he chooses to smoke a cigarette, high up in the Andes, where the air is thin and breathing troublesome? Besides, with all the political turmoil that's going on, why would anyone want to pay a call on death? If you're feeling like a daredevil, try to jaywalk across *La Avenida Arequipa*. Sneak out during curfew. Try eating one of those *ceviches* sold in plastic bags by beach *ambulantes* in the summertime.

I don't know what to think at times. Especially after watching how the smoker comes to a complete standstill in order to be able to cough more easily. It doesn't help. The cough is loud, dry and uncontrollable. If anything, the halt has made it worse. Left with no choice, he decides to do what any educated man would do in this situation: have a drink. He wastes no time, once more reaching his hands deep into the pockets of his Outer Tactical Vest. The search lasts until a facial expression of relief lets us know he's found what he's looking for.

What he pulls out – a 975[23] sterling silver hand-carved flask with another *Tumi* engraved on the side – comes as no surprise. What truly amazes us is the repetitive theme of the *Tumi*. He's a *Sinchi* – a warrior. The *Tumi* was a type of knife used by the Incas to slit the throats of captives. Perhaps this is the struggle this man is facing: to be honourable or not. As he begins to take a few long swigs from his canteen, I begin to wonder what the outcome will be.

Mucus, blood, and small particles that were lodged in his throat and lungs are loosened. He starts sneezing. He makes gargling sounds to further loosen the lodged fragments. He spits. Gargles. Spits. The result of this continual grooming process makes his voice audible, as his Lima accent rises like a condor over the horizon, 'This place is such a shithole! No schools. No churches. No markets. No roads. Marched for two days. Nonstop. Aj! Just for this? Fuck!'

Putting his hands on his sides and bending forward, the *Sinchi* tries to dislodge any remaining particles. He resembles a pecking chicken. Breath in. Phlegm out. Breath in. Phlegm out. Possessed, as if in a trance. The quicker he does it the more it looks like a ritualistic dance. And it succeeds, as Pariacaca blesses the land with drizzle.

Feeling the first drops on his face, he pauses. Spits. Stands up straight. Turns his head towards the heavens, as if to ask why. Trying to take a few steps forward, the *Sinchi* accidentally slips onto his knees. Covered from the waist down in mud he addresses the town, 'I know you're hiding! Come out and face me like a man! Sons of bitches! Quit hiding in your houses with your livestock. Smelling alike. Speaking the same fucking language! I begin to wonder what the hell you *comuneros* are doing, hiding all cosy under your mattresses with your animals? I know you can hear me. Answer me! Now!'

Rising up like a phoenix from its ashes, he decides not to waste his time by scraping the mud off, acting as if it were a blessing by Pachamama. Once again, he does what any man would do in this situation: reaches for a smoke. Feeling up the contour of a pocket from his moist Outer Tactical Vest, in the same way a man feels up a woman, he searches for the packet of rolling paper. Finding it damp, he grunts and tries the other pocket until a smoker's cough causes him to rethink his vice.

Realising the lack of oxygen might have something to do with it, he decides to walk off his cough and heads towards the wall of the nearest house. However, he falls well short of his goal and leans against the first sizeable object he can find. A boulder. Placed there by time. Serving no particular purpose. Turned hammock.

During this bout of breathlessness the *Sinchi* began to realise that losing his patience has made his smoker's cough harder to tame and catching his breath harder work, 'Okay! Okay! I get it. I keep on forgetting that I'm not in Lima anymore. The air is paper-thin. If you breathe it in too quickly, your lungs feel as if they were paper cutouts.'

For the first time in his whole soliloquy, the man pauses out of self-awareness. He makes an almost 360-degree turn to check if anyone can hear him. As a member of a special task force known for committing unspeakable acts of violence, you wouldn't want your squadron to think that you're not right in the head. Would you?

Automatic weapons. Grenades. Knives. Handguns. Wire cutters. Cyanide. Interrogation techniques. Friendly fire. Killing children. Raping women. Dismembering elders. Raping men. Executing POWs. Stealing cattle. Burning down houses. Digging mass graves. Filling them. Disappearing people. Beating. Intimidating. Amputating. Waterboarding. And all of a sudden you, a *Sinchi* of all people, are somehow concerned with what a fellow troop member or official might think of you. Please!

Breaking out of his verbal trance, the man shakes his head, laughs out loud to himself, and then returns once again to externalising his thoughts to the local cattle, 'Thank you. Thank you. You have all been a lovely audience tonight. Honestly. Yes, you! Thank you. Thank you. Next week I'll be in Las Vegas performing live with Dean Martin from Caesar's Pala...'

Like a deflating balloon, the man pauses. He hears marching. As if in slow motion, a platoon of about seven men approach. They seem to take an eternity to reach him. It's almost like watching a fly resisting gale-force winds. His galloping heart and overheated nerves begin to play tricks on him. Did they hear, or worse, see anything?

Internal lightning bolts of panic run up and down his body. He can't even move. He must not show fear. His body makes its subconscious attempt to bluff its way out of danger by playing it cool. Rigid – like the lampposts where the dogs were hung – his eyes, not him, watch the troop come and go.

Saved by a hair's breadth. The *Sinchi* releases a fart of relief, as if sending Pariacaca a telegraph to thank her for his good fortune. No need for good luck charms like *huayruros*[24]. Maybe the Inca gods have spared him because they see a true warrior in him. A *Sinchi*. Not just another person holding a *Tumi*'s blade at someone's throat. Ascended to Heaven. Returned to Earth three days later. He's become another one of the Holy Ghosts of Peru. A *desaparecido*.

But once you've disappeared, you can never come back. When the seven men reached him, instead of coming to a complete stop, they partially slowed down, turned towards him, and saluted him, before passing by. They have seen him. The problem is that he hasn't seen himself.

On the one hand, what we've learned from the exchange of hand gestures is that the *Sinchi* must be an officer of rank because the lowest rank always salutes the higher ranks first; while on the other hand, maybe becoming one of the Holy Ghosts means that a part of him has been extirpated. Like a Catholic confessing and taking communion, it only works if you keep on doing it. Without these sacraments, the soul is unable to let the Saviour in. Perhaps that is his problem. He has stopped. No god has been in him for so long that a part of him has died, and that is always a dangerous thing to find in a man: the lack of god.

And godless is the greenness of mountains. Fake. Like surgically enhanced breasts. And godless are the extreme temperature fluctuations. Low wind-chills mixed with a high UV index. A scorched-like crisp feel to a land that wears a light brown hue: the colour of an ailing person. And godless are the mountain crests. White. Grey. Like hair on an old man's head. Full of wisdom and death, the *Cordillera* is waiting to be reburied back at sea. And godless are we, doomed to sit here and watch.

The troop now out of sight, the officer – with a little smile on his face – decides to recommence his sermon, but this time he addresses the mountains instead of the animals, 'No running water. No roads. No education. No electricity. No employment. No opportunities. I can see why they call this place Ayacucho. This is death's corner in more than one way. The dead end of civilisation. I imagine this is where the Catholic Church sends their troublesome priests to find salvation and compassion amongst those who are doomed to hell twice...'

Pausing to see if there was a church around the town centre, he sees none. Smiles. Makes the sign of the cross on a nearby stone, as if this gesture erected a cathedral. Smiles again by lifting his head skyward. Then, bows his head. Makes the sign of the cross again. His prayer is finished. Maybe God will save these people now. Or at least I think that this is what he wants.

Finding a sense of inner peace, he closes his eyes much like some musicians do when they sing and says to himself out loud, 'I'm no missionary and no *conquistador*. I'll do my duty, but I won't.'

Without warning, a lowly foot soldier startles the officer by sneaking up behind him, tapping him on his left shoulder. More stirred up than a coffee with milk and two sugars, the officer opens his eyes so wide that it seems like they're going to pop right out of his face, throwing his arms and legs out like a falling cat. His feet land on a nearby pile of shit. What type? As I have said before, it doesn't matter. Whether some smells worse than others, shit is shit. Undesirable. Unwanted. Unable to scrape it off his boots with a simple twig like the last time.

Once he regains some sense of composure, he turns around, looks at the foot soldier and shouts *a voz de cuerda*, 'You son of a bitch! Fuck! Me! What kind of a fucking moron are you? Are we not fighting a war? Does this look like the place to play jokes?'

In a low, squeaky voice, with his head bowed on his hands like a repentant Catholic, the soldier excuses himself.

'That is the one thing you are not: excused! And is it me or aren't you addressing an officer?'

Changing his tone, the soldier speaks in a more assertive, military-like voice. The officer begins to squeeze the soldier's shoulder tighter and tighter, as if through pain – in the same way one domesticates an animal – the soldier will understand who's really running the show.

Bending over, with his hands around the sides of his waist, the officer begins to throw up a dark mucus-like substance, a combination of stomach acid and stomach lining. This time everything that was lodged in his upper body has come loose. No need for a swig of home-made Pisco. He heads for the next best medicine: cigarettes.

Noticing that the envelope of tobacco and foreign rolling paper are still wet, he improvises by looking for the nearest dry surface. Once he's found it, he takes out what seems to be a map of the region of Ayacucho and spreads it on a rock, as if it were a tablecloth covering a fancy marble counter. Then he takes out all the cigarette stubs, which he kept in his innermost pocket, and proceeds to extract what little tobacco he can find in each, one by one.

Surprisingly, his addiction has provided him with enough to fill three cigarettes. He carefully begins to stuff the tobacco he doesn't need somewhere in between the back pages of his notebook while at the same time trying to pour the correct amount onto the cover. Like Peruvian doctors, known around the world for their ability to improvise, he takes a 10,000 *Intis* note from his wallet – which by now is worth as much as toilet paper after this month's inflation – and lays it out flat next to the tobacco.

Laughing, he loads one side of the rectangular banknote with the compacted, cylinder-like bundle of nightshade he's collected. Then, rolling his precious fatty with all the precision of a brain surgeon, the officer licks it until the moist ciggie is welded together by saliva. Giving it some time to dry, he proceeds to carefully tear out a corner from the cover page of his notebook. Rolling it into a filter, much like a *pastelero* makes cocaine paste, he adds the final touch by jamming it into one end. And *voila*! Breakfast is served.

No need for a coffee. He holds his pastry in between his lips and searches for his beloved *Tumi*-engraved Zippo lighter by feeling up his Outer Tactile Vest the same way he would pleasure his beloved. But the orgasm does not come until he finds it, extracts it from his pocket, and lights up his fag. The feast, the fix, the fuck, begins.

One puff, all is forgotten. Two puffs, all is restored. From there on, all is good. No half-wit *soldado*. No stupid questions. No thinking about the surrounding nothingness. The clouds of smoke bring back memories of Lima. Like a shaman, suddenly he foresees life here. It's hidden, but it's here. Waiting to be found. And just as its location was about to be revealed, Pariacaca sent a gust of wind like a telegram, distorting the village's image. What he saw resembled the Tower card in a Tarot pack: a crumbling building on fire, agonising screams, and dead bodies. But what did it all mean?

Confused, he decides with the final puff of his cigarette to return to his speech as if nothing had happened, 'Of all the things I've seen so far, what has troubled me the most was that land divider I saw earlier on. What's the fucking point? All this open land and that's it! No wonder there's barely enough food to go around in the provinces. Squalid. Stupid. If someone stole your food, you'd know: they'd be the only ones not chewing coca leaves to suppress hunger.'

Out of nowhere comes a firm hand that taps the officer's shoulder from behind. Startled. He turns with the force of a lightning bolt. He lets out a scream that paralyses the entire village and almost collapses his lungs, 'You fucking, dumb, son of a bitch! What did I tell you last time *soldado*? I thought I told you never to...'

Before he could finish his last insult, he realises that it's not the same soldier. Clearing his throat. Appearing apologetic. After an exchange of salutes, the conversation takes a more relaxed tone. At one point, the *Sinchi* reaches for his handgun and releases the safety catch. The soldier quietly walks away with his head down. However, something lingers in the *Sinchi*'s mind. The thought of his past life. One that he knows he'll never be able to return to.

Banishment. Crumbling. Burning. Dying. It seems those images he saw earlier in his cloud of cigarette smoke have partly come true. What if the Tarot card were upside down, though? The tower of his life's work is collapsing. Like the burning of the books in Nazi Germany, the knowledge in his head is fading little by little. A part of him was dying. Consumed by the flames of war. The country was crumbling. Would there be a chance for a new beginning? Though the Tarot cards might say yes, life has a strange way of saying no.

As a way of both escaping his innermost thoughts and killing time before his approaching meeting, the *Sinchi* decides to return to his earlier soliloquy. However, unlike previous attempts, this time the words flow without thought. He's like a lecturer addressing a classroom once again. 'As I was saying earlier on, after all I've thus far seen, I cannot get my head around why the *comuneros* choose to live like this. Chewing coca and working their shit-covered fields to barely make ends meet. They have no light, water or gas bills to pay; rent due at the end of the month; cars to maintain, gasoline to buy or taxes to declare; probably even currency. Yet they are suffering from the same problems we are in Lima. Food shortages. Uncertainty. No opportunities. Inequality. Terror. You begin to wonder who are the ones who are really being left out in the dark. Maybe Lima's got it all wrong. Maybe, I… '

After pausing for a moment to regain his breath, the *Sinchi* begins to realise what he's saying. These are thoughts contrary to his sense of duty. Thoughts of sedition. Contrary opinions. Are these his thoughts?

Trying to find a way to vent his anger – one that will not worsen his breathlessness and uncontrollable cough – the *Sinchi* tries to find a balance. However, he is unable to do so. Too much self-reflection is not good for a man. His hands run wild around the pockets of his Outer Tactile Vest. Rummaging for another fix. Only this time, he's out of money to burn.

Desperation leads to trembling. Trembling makes him forget about the flask of Pisco. He begins to study the scenery like a Romantic poet, trying to draw a sense of calmness and inspiration from it, 'Here I feel disconnected from everything. That is probably why I am feeling so confused these days. In Lima, there is no choice. The battles go on. People are forced to fight.'

'Instead, I am here. Surrounded by nature. Forced to acknowledge what is in front of me, regardless of personal choice. I begin to wonder: what am I actually fighting for? Who am I fighting for? Is it for Peru? Lima? Those fucking ignorant *cholos de mierda*[25]? Why did I leave my post at the university? I'm supposed to teach the young, not kill them. What the fuck was I thinking? Honestly! I'm the last person in Lima, Peru, the entire world who should be...'

Not knowing what to think, not knowing what to do, the *Sinchi* decides to go for a walk without caring about where he is heading. This time, it's not the mouth which is leading him; rather, it's the body that's doing all the talking. Cigarette-less. He reaches into one of his innermost breast pockets and pulls out his notebook. He rips out two of the thickest pages he can find. He sits down on a random rock to roll himself a cigarette. Using the same technique as last time, he pulls out the notebook once again, opening it on the page where he has stashed his tobacco like a hidden exclamation mark. Having filled each of the small sheets of paper with equal amounts of tobacco, he rolls them up one at a time. Using his saliva as an adhesive bond, the *Sinchi* stuffs the filters with two small pieces from the cover of his notebook.

His precious cigarettes now finished, he carefully places the notebook back into his innermost breast pocket, kissing it with gratitude. The kiss of gratitude you would give to a call girl rather than your wife. He stands up from the rock murmuring to himself, 'This one is for now. The other, for when I'm done with this place.'

Carefully placing one of the two cigarettes into an empty pocket, he reaches for his lighter, places the third cigarette in his mouth, and begins to indulge. It seems that his breathing has not been worsened by his bad habits. Taking one final 360-degree look at his surroundings, he carries on with his ambulatory soliloquy, 'In all fairness, even if I wanted to reason with them, how could I? Most of the *comuneros* cannot speak a word of *castellano*, let alone read or write. I mean, what else could I expect from a place with no newspapers, books, radio, television…'

'Besides, how could one bring the modernity of Lima to the provinces, even if one wanted to? Electricity, construction materials and technology is one thing, but education, manners and etiquette is… What am I saying! It's just absolutely impossible. It can't be done.'

His cigarette was finished. Away went his calmness. His reasoning skills. The last puff stole the human being out of him.

Before the *Sinchi* has reached the edge of town he finds himself bending over with his hands on his stomach, throwing up everything he has in him. Pisco. Cigarette smoke. Stomach acid. Black mucus. Undigested, reconstituted meat from the day before. And blood. He knows how lucky he is not to have been seen in this delirious state by any of his *soldados*. He makes the pact with himself not to have another one of his fits of rage.

Only a few more hours and he'll be on his way with his men to the capital of Ayacucho. Only a few more hours and he can smoke his victory cigar. Only a few more hours! Having said that, a minute can sometimes feel like a day. Especially out here, far from the grip of minute and second hands. The thought of meeting up with a supply group waiting for him with more Pisco and cigarettes gives him the strength to continue.

After incorporating himself and using a nearby twig to wipe any large chunks of mud off the soles of his boots, the *Sinchi* begins to walk back to the village where his men are waiting for him alongside a group of rounded up *comuneros*. Every other step is followed by a corresponding inhalation or exhalation in an attempt to regulate his breathing. It takes about a half a lap around an imaginary track for him to start breathing normally. Composure returns little by little with each subsequent breath.

However, he is down to his last bullet: one cigarette. It is not as if he can just walk away in the middle of an operation to talk to himself, throw a fit, vomit, drink, smoke or calm himself down. When you're at work, you can't just walk it off. You have to reason your way out of it. Formerly as a don, he had been able to do as he pleased both in and out of his classroom; he no longer feels capable of such arrogant behaviour. Perhaps the only things the *Sinchi* had left behind in his academic life were a desk, false praise, a red marker, chalk and the advantages of having the abbreviation 'Dr'. Everything else is still in him, though not in the way he wishes.

By the time he is done reflecting on his life, the *Sinchi* finds himself approaching the *Plaza de Armas* – or what his lieutenant deems to be so. Edged by two dozen crumbling adobe huts with mouldy straw roofs, broken wooden shutters and oddly coloured front doors made from dyes of plants and animal blood, the square stinks of putrefying corpses.

However, Pachamama is probably the only one of the visitors who is not bothered by the putrefying smell of gut-based paints or the decaying housing. Everything here is natural. Returning to the land. Perhaps, this is a way for the *comuneros* to thank her. What is used is paid back, so it can return in another form.

Everything here expresses a sense of harmony, of flow. The *Sinchis* are nothing like that. They dress in black: the colour that absorbs all light, the colour of death and unpredictability. They wear nothing natural. Eat reconstituted foods. Trash everything. Rape. Kill their own kind. Carry weapons capable of a level and rapidity of destruction that would take Pachamama and her siblings months of planning to equal. Maybe that is why Pariacaca was crying earlier on: she knew what was to come.

Returning to that nauseating smell; it resembles the foul smells found in Lima. The smell of exhaust from cars that fail the national technical revision, but by means of bribery are still out on the roads, staining the white walls, tiles, and billboards of the city with carbon monoxide. The smell of fish mills in August covering the coast with an invisible layer of burning and disturbance. The smell of the ocean, glossed with tonnes of illegal chemicals. The smells of alleys covered in piss, shit, trash, vomit and an occasional dead house pet some parent did not want their children to find.

The fact of the matter is, what most resembles Lima is not the smell. It is the small-scale urbanisation that the *comuneros* have applied. At the centre of town, there is a large church-like building, probably built by visiting missionaries. This structure brings a wide smile to the *Sinchi*'s face.

When I say churchlike, what I really mean to say is that this structure was more of a humble community hall. *La Municipalidad.* Though, the reason I think it's a church is because its crumbling edifice is held together by an inexplicable faith, a miracle. Somehow the slanted walls, their holes visibly patched with dirt, still stand like a valiant *Sinchi* holding down the fort despite the odds.

Yet the most curious detail about this 'church' is what surrounds it. This Sistine Chapel of poverty is enclosed by a solitary Inca-like stone wall about two metres high – whose purpose is unknown – although if you saw it you'd probably think it was the identical twin of the Wailing Wall in Israel. You'd feel almost obliged to fill its nooks and cracks with a prayer note, or at the very least have a yeshiva student place one for you. That is, if you could persuade one of them to go there.

You would wonder what they built this wall for. Sacrifice? Postings? Protection? It surely wasn't built for keeping thieves out of the *Municipalidad* since the opening on both sides has no doors. Whatever it was built for, you'd think sooner or later someone would have found a new use for it.

The second level of urbanisation is a compacted dirt road, probably flattened by a horse pulling a homemade plough. Surprisingly, it is very firm. Almost like concrete. It is also very wide, like the *Champs-Élysées*. The only thing that's missing is an *Arc de Triomphe*.

The third and final tier is composed of four blocks of six houses. Each block has two rows of three houses which have the Haussmann or Parisian touch of being identical, built in the same style and from the same materials as the churchlike central structure. Each of the four blocks forms an arm of the compass. North. South. East. West. Each of the four blocks is also divided by four roads which commence at the central circular road and lead outward. For a group of people who were labelled as ignorant, they put a lot more urban planning into their city than the inhabitants of Lima ever did.

And it was here, somewhere in between the edge of the road and the wall, that about three dozen soldiers stand, mingling with the *comuneros*. The contrast between the *Sinchis* and the *comuneros* is remarkable. On the one hand, most of the *Sinchis* are neatly shaved, wear new clothes, smell good, possess modern weaponry, are well fed and speak more or less eloquently; while the *comuneros* are un-shaven, smell terrible, and wear patched rags that cling to their skins and whatever bulk they still have.

However, what truly differentiates the two groups the most are their respective weap-ons. Those of the *comuneros* are locally made, feeble and unmenacing. In comparison, the *Sinchis'* hardware is from a different planet. When the *Sinchi* approaches the circular road the entire village goes silent. Even the *co-muneros* know he is the man they are waiting for. And as he is the *capac* or warlord of his tribe, out of respect, not a sound is made.

Maybe it is the way he presents himself which leads to such reverence by the *comuneros*. Un-like his companions, the *Sinchi* is in his late forties. His skin is European white. Clear eyes. Short hair. Thin. Well-trimmed. Good posture. Height about six feet. The only thing he is missing is a moustache; otherwise he has all the attributes of an aristocratic man. That and the fact that he is in the provinces. It is strange to see a man of his dignity in such a place. After all, a high-ranking official would never be sent on such a basic combat mission, let alone to rural Peru. Nevertheless, these are times of war, and experience is always welcomed by the armed forces.

Everything leading up to this moment feels as if it has originated in a magical realist novel. Bullshit. Descriptive. Exaggerated. We are accomplices, covered in shit. What type? It doesn't matter, because shit is shit. And being full of it is just as bad. That is why what is to happen from now on can only be described as realism: the reality of things. Shaman or no shaman, the rabbit has been pulled out of the hat one too many times, killing the magical.

After acknowledging his troops with a salute, the *Sinchi* walks up towards the crowd, stopping a few metres shy. Finding a sizeable stone that probably once belonged to one of the surrounding buildings, he steps on top of it. Like a man in need of a balcony to make a speech, he clears his throat and smiles, as if to reinstate calm amongst the spectators.

As a means of showing a link of trust and respect between the *comuneros*, he salutes them before beginning his introductory address, '*Buenos días a todos*. I have come here on behalf of both the Peruvian Army and Government as part of their efforts to suppress the *Senderista* uprising.'

'Many of you are probably already familiar with the *Senderista* tactics. That is why I've come to you, my fellow *comuneros* and *ronderos*, as a sign of trust, solidarity, and respect. And it is with those virtues in mind that I ask you all to please collaborate with me, in our efforts to free these lands of this menace. So, if any of you are willing, I would be most grateful if you could please give me your full cooperation by...'

The *soldado* who interrupts the *Sinchi* has a half-Limenean, half-Andean complexion. He enters the *Plaza de Armas* accompanied by a group of *comuneros* who resemble him: a few young men holding homemade farming equipment and an elderly man using a mouldy tree branch as a walking stick to balance his ageing swagger.

Now that everyone is in place, the soldier addresses the *Sinchi* after saluting him. 'Sir, what else should we do with the *comuneros*? Sir!'

'Could I please inspect your sidearm, Quispe?'

Quispe carefully takes out his sidearm, walks up to the *Sinchi* and hands it over handle first, 'Sir! Yes, sir!'

Accepting the sidearm, the *Sinchi* grips it correctly, pulls the safety catch, and aims it at Quispe's temple, 'First of all, an officer never surrenders his sidearm. Then again, you never were much of a soldier, or a man, for that matter.'

The *Sinchi*, still aiming the sidearm at *soldado* Quispe's temple, pulls the trigger, but the clicking sound yields no bullet, 'Sometimes a *cholo de mierda* is tougher to kill than a colony of cockroaches. But who knows, the third time tends to be *la vencida*.'

Because in Latin America we are superstitious, we avoid saying *the third time's the charm*. Rather, we say *la tercera es la vencida*. Quispe knew he was a bit of both. Shook up.

Knowing he can do what he wants with Quispe – well, at least psychologically, since the gun he's holding is out of bullets, and beating him with the handle is too laborious – the *Sinchi* proceeds to berate the soldier.

Knowing well that the *Sinchi* is just looking for an excuse to draw his sidearm, which is only inches away, Quispe reacts with words of praise for the *Sinchi*, and utter humiliation for himself, '*Si mi coronel*, you are right: I will wait for your orders from now on. Let me go join the cattle to make sure those dumb fucks stay in line. *Permiso, mi coronel*!'

Following another meaningless exchange of salutes, the *Sinchi* steps back on top of his rocky podium. After a few seconds he addresses the crowd again, 'Well, as I was saying to you, your cooperation with respect to the whereabouts of the terrorists would be of great use to me. Especially in our recent efforts to exterminate the root of the problem'.

Not a single sound can be heard. Even the wind has died down. The *Sinchi* does not know how to react to the poker faces of the *comuneros*. It begins to look as if he's called their bluff and they have replied by raising the stakes. It's the *Sinchi*'s turn to call and raise since thus far he's not been able to get his message through to them. Although with that 'exterminate': was it a Freudian slip?

Maybe it's time for the good cop, bad cop approach.

So, the *Sinchi* tries for a more sympathetic approach by widening his smile, loosening up his body language, and adding some gestures to aid his efforts through recognisable visual mannerisms.

The good cop approach is met just like previously: by an omnipotent silence that envelops the village faster than a quake. Even the animals are silent. It's as if the lungs of the world, which are the Andes, can be heard breathing.

We have somehow returned to that void where we began this tale.

The blankness has an adverse effect on the *Sinchi*. He's perplexed. He wonders how he should approach the *comuneros*. Maybe he was right: they are like animals. However, even animals can be domesticated. This does not seem to be the case here.

Realising that it's perhaps too soon to become the bad cop, the *Sinchi* opts to try a more fatherly tone. But the repetitive silence starts to wear down the *Sinchi*'s spirit – which is that of a compulsive gambler, someone who likes repeatedly to roll the dice of chance just one more time, using any number of gesticulations, props and simple words to get his point across. Now he is prompted into using baby talk, 'I am *Sinchi*. Gooooood *Sinchi*.

You are *comuneros*. You live here. You help me. Then good *Sinchi* find *Senderistas*. *Senderistas* bad *Sinchis*! We find bad *Sinchis*. Where are the bad...'

The *Sinchi* has had enough of silence. Fuck the bad cop routine. What they need is badass. And that means it's time for a little head bashing. Army style. No rules. No mercy. No human rights, because in this country they have been indefinitely suspended. In other words, whatever happens during the Internal Conflict remains part of the Internal Conflict. Guaranteed. Does this sound familiar to you?

The veins on the *Sinchi*'s face and neck are starting to pop out, purplish, not red, as if they were varicose. His eyes are as wide as the view itself. His blood pressure is off the monitor scale and his lips are wobbling in a strange way. Hands trembling. With one hand on his holster, he further raises his tone.

Believe it or not, the *Sinchi* is interrupted once again by the gambler of all gamblers, *soldado* Quispe, 'Sir, I think the problem is that most of the *comuneros* um… I mean the animals only speak Quechua, if anything at all resembling a language. Would you like me to translate into Ayacuchan Quechua what you've been saying, sir?'

Exhausted. Irritated. Irrational. The *Sinchi* unstraps the M16 assault rifle hanging over his shoulders and in a fit of rage releases a round onto a side of the stone wall.

The finger-sized bullets pierce into the stone, as if kissing the boulders with the soft caresses of attrition, just a few feet short of wiping out the crowd. So much for the Quispe School of Diplomacy. The rest of the subordinate *Sinchi* officers remain locked in position.

Children begin to cry. Mothers grow restless. Men quiver at the awesome power of an unfamiliar automatic weapon. Everyone seems in a state of shock, except for the old man with a mouldy stick for a cane who seems to be comforted by the prospect of a quick death. It seems the *Sinchi* might be the answer to the prayer of his crumbling bones, reduced by time to a gelatine-like substance.

His temper tantrum over, the *Sinchi* turns towards Quispe with the full intention of committing murder one.

With the biggest smile you've ever seen, the *Sinchi* hands his sidearm to Quispe, who inspects the gun. Once he's verified that there's only one bullet in the cylinder, he places the barrel above his right ear and turns to the *Sinchi*, 'When should I pull the trigger, *coronel*?'

'On the count of three.'

'*Si, coronel*!'

'Do you wish to say any final words, just in case, *soldado* Quispe?'

'*Si, coronel*!'

'And what have you to say?'

'Tell the President that I send him my regards.'

'One… Two… Three!'

Right before pulling the trigger, Quispe euphorically shouts what appears to be his philosophy: '*Viva la revolución*!'

Bang! But there is no bang. Quispe is shaken but unharmed. The *Sinchi* is both perplexed and indignant at Quispe's luck. Turning around with a defiant smile only the *comuneros* and a few *soldados* could see, the *Sinchi* looks

as if he has had just about enough. He's so an-
gry that this time he forgets about his stone
podium. Fuck it. He approaches the crowd,
standing only inches away from those in the
front row and announces, 'I am officially
done playing fucking games with you. I don't
care if you don't speak *castellano*. I don't care
if you pretend not to speak *castellano*. I don't
care if you don't want to speak *castellano*.
Though I can tell you one thing for sure: hell
will freeze over before I make an attempt at
speaking a word of Quechua.'

He could not tell if it was his recent sequence
of menacing actions, his latest speech or the
word Quechua, but all of a sudden he detect-
ed a flicker of their attention.

But besides the odd sound of a *comunero*
chewing coca to suppress hunger, nothing
could be heard. All they seemed capable of
doing was standing up as straight and silent as
a guard outside the National Palace.

The unsuccessful attempts made by the *Sinchi* to persuade the *comuneros* to talk could lead us to three conclusions. One: the mathematical impossibility of dividing a number by zero is false, as the nothingness of the morning divided by the nothingness of their response leads to a nothing so silent that it is deafening. Two: the stalemate between the *Sinchi* and the *comuneros* is Zeno's Paradox come to life: each approach gets only halfway, leaving another half to go. Three: if the *Sinchi* were into human resources, he would have discovered the *comuneros'* third employable skill besides standing still and remaining silent: indifference. And this was a very Limenean skill to possess at the time.

Actually, now that I think of it, points one and two are bullshit. They sounded better in my head than on paper; however, I just thought I'd mention what's on my mind. Something real. Instead of sounding like I'm full of shit. That's what it was: a friendly gesture aimed at breaking the ice, seeing as silence is in abundance today. I bet the *Sinchi* would have given up his last cigarette just to hear one of the *comuneros* say anything at all. A thought. A word. A gesture. Even a *fuck you* sounded better than putting up with more of this nerve-racking nothingness.

Although the *Sinchi* thinks of loading up his M16 and releasing round after round of middle finger sized bullets on the *comuneros*, he realises that by doing so, he will have wasted an entire morning. And it is the thought of adding more nothingness to the existing nothingness which drives him, towards the techniques the *Sinchis* are notorious for.

Pointing his finger at random, it lands on a group of about four soldiers, '*Soldados*! Yes, you lot. How about you four and that fucking prick Quispe, wherever he is, start to round up as many children as you can find. In the mean time, can somebody bring me that old man over there? The one who uses a tree branch as a walking stick. Yes, that one!'

'Sir! Yes, sir!'

While the four soldiers round up the children, Quispe directs himself to where the old man is standing in the hope that obedience and determination might lead towards leniency for his client. So, whispering something into the man's ear, Quispe stands behind him and symbolically points his gun at the back of the old man's neck in what could only be called typical *Sinchi* fashion.

In Latin America, it is rumoured that the warmth of its people make it a desirable destination. However, the way in which the four soldiers opt to gather the children expresses a syndrome of revolution and hatred that tends to manifest itself around the continent every fifty years or so. They pull a few of the children by their hair. Beat some out of their mother's arms. Fire warning shots into the air to frighten parents away. Spitting. Swearing. Punching. The only thing they stop short of is raping or killing, but that's only because their commander is waiting for them.

Though what is most disconcerting about the whole scene is that the old man, who is missing half his teeth, smiles gaily in the midst of all this terror as he hobbles towards the *Sinchi*. Once the old man reaches his destination, Quispe carefully lowers his weapon and helps him onto the stone where the *Sinchi* had been standing to make his speeches. Turning his focus towards the old man, the *Sinchi* begins by formally addressing himself to his captive, 'Good day, sir. May I ask you a few questions?'

For whatever inexplicable reason, the old man nods back to the *Sinchi*, as if saying yes.

'Well sir, I am a *Sinchi* and...'

The old man interrupts him, as if posing a question while making a flapping gesture with his hands and then pointing up towards the sky, '*Manam pisqo?*'

The *Sinchi* tries to figure out what he is saying while not losing his patience at the fact that he's been interrupted yet again.

'Please excuse me good sir, but might I ask what your name is?'

Silence.

Giving a polite smile and using any number of gesticulations, 'I'm going to assume you couldn't hear me, so, I'll ask again sir! What … is … your … name … please?'

The man's inability or unwillingness to answer the simplest of questions sends the *Sinchi* into a rage. He takes out his revolver, loads it, and points the barrel at the man's head.

Shrugging his shoulders, the old man replies, '*Manam Cayitsu.*'

'Finally: some progress! It seems you do speak some *castellano* after all, Mr *Cayitsu*. I apologise for the intimidation, but there's no harm in a little conversation starter, is there? Well, as I was asking your fellow *comuneros*: do you have any information you'd like to share, concerning the *Senderistas*? Remember my oath of discretion: whatever's said here, stays here.'

'*Manam Cayitsu.*'

Almost laughing, 'Sir, I already know your name; however, what I would like to know is...'

Again, *soldado* Quispe insists on interrupting his superior officer to make his opinion known, '*Coronel*, what the man is trying to say is...'

Before Quispe can even finish his sentence, the *Sinchi* approaches him, almost stepping over the old man.

The *Sinchi* takes the safety catch off his weapon and with the smallest of sounds, a click, he manages to turn the expression on Quispe's face three hundred and sixty degrees around.

Once the *Sinchi's* finished with what he believes is putting Quispe in his place once and for all, he heads back to where he left the old man sitting on his eternal stage of stone, 'Now … as I was um … saying: what I want to … know from you is …'

'*Manam Cayitsu.*'

The *Sinchi* takes his revolver out of its holster and aims the tip of the barrel at the old man's mouth, 'The next couple of fucking words coming out of your mouth, better not be your name, or I swear I'll blow your fucking head off! Where are the *Senderistas*? Now!!!'

The old man is not shaken at all by the *Sinchi*'s threats; rather, he seems quite content to take this conversation to the next level. He remains silent. This forces the *Sinchi* to push the barrel, little by little, into the old man's mouth. The old man stares at the mountains where he has lived his entire life and the *Sinchi* stands still, silent, with a blank look, as if he had disappeared.

'The *coronel comunero*', he thinks to himself, as he stands with him.

It's the old man who provides us with the icebreaker. Perhaps a coward at heart, unable to take his own life, he seems poised to make the most of this opportunity. He defiantly moves towards the *Sinchi*, one wobbly step at a time. It's as if he is begging to be killed.

Once he makes it to within a foot of the *Sinchi*'s face, he stops and shouts at the top of his lungs while holding on to his walking stick for dear life, '*Manam Cayitsu*!'

The *Sinchi* strikes the man to the ground with his fists and shouts, 'I've had enough of your Quechuan bullshit, you dumb old cunt! Look at what you're making me do! Don't you realise!? I never asked for this. We can both put an end to all of this shit. Just fucking tell me where the *Senderistas* are. Now!!!'

In a quivering voice the old man utters what may well be his final words, '*Manam Cayitsu*.'

Deciding that sometimes there's a fate crueller than death, the *Sinchi* decides to point the old man's attention towards the children that are being rounded up. Once he's sure he has the old man's focus, he takes out his revolver and aims it at them.

The old man's face expresses horror as he realises what is about to happen. He tries to muster all of his strength, before releasing his verbal warning shot, but it is intercepted by the *Sinchi* who beats the old man with the butt of his gun. All that can be heard from the old man before he's out cold is a faint, '*Manam pisqo.*'

Limenean shaman. Literary clairvoyant. Part-time *curandero*. The only moment of magical realism that can be attributed to recent events was the *Sinchi*'s bizarre decision to pick up the old man's mouldy walking stick and wave it like a baton.

Speechless. Motionless. Breathless. The *co-muneros* interpret the *Sinchi*'s actions as those of a *paco*[26] before making payment to Pachamama. Perhaps, that helps to explain why no one bothers to complain. Or flinch. He resembles a *Sinchi* or Inca priest, pulling out his *Tumi* and slicing open his prisoners' throats. What if all the *Sinchi* has really done is signal that the time for a sacrifice has come?

Whether we can use this gesture as a *mullu* to predict events is difficult to tell. The *comuneros* live and pray off the land. They're used to this sort of behaviour. The irrational is rational here where magic is a reality in and of itself.

Dogs or no dogs hanging, be it Lima or Huánuco, magic is a part of their life. It can't be killed! Despite military, paramilitary and terrorist forces trying their best. All one can do is adapt to one's surroundings. And this is Ayacucho: death's corner. Where people magically disappear.

Becoming visible was never a problem for the *Sinchi*. Following his athletic display, he proceeded to go back to his place on top of his stone podium. From there he readdressed the *comuneros* as if nothing had happened.

By now, it is obvious that the *Sinchi* is flustered. Nothing seems to work. It's as if everyone shared the same wish as the old man to die. Kamikazes. What means are used to justify their ends do not matter. Plus, the *Sinchi* is aware that language is neither a barrier nor the root of the problem.

Perhaps the notion of the inevitable has something to do with it. Sooner or later, someone else will come and threaten their way of life. It is just a matter of time. They are too far behind the times. Too isolated. Too exposed to the elements. Hence, choice – that of whether or not to surrender, to collaborate, to unite – becomes their only weapon. And it's exactly that: their choice to remain silent, which the *Sinchi* cannot seem to overcome.

As usual, it's the innocent who pay the price. About a dozen children have been rounded up. To really hit your enemy, you have to hit them where it hurts the most.

'From what I gather, no one has anything they want to tell me. Well, let me see what I can do to loosen your tongues a bit. *Soldados*! Yes, you four: line up all the children you've managed to gather and put them over there, backs against the stone wall. Then, wait for my command.'

As the *soldados* round the children up, the *Sinchi* remarks, 'I guess we're about to find out very quickly just how silent you sons of bitches intend to remain. So, out of politeness, I'm going to ask you all, one more time: does anyone have anything they'd like to share with me? Anybody? Anything?'

As the *Sinchi* gets off the stone, and heads towards the four *soldados*, he murmurs to himself, 'Poor miserable bastards! May God have mercy on their souls.'

When the *Sinchi* reaches the four of them, he places himself to their left, at about the same height. It seems the *soldados* know exactly what to do, as they line up side by side. In the meantime, the children are leaning against the wall thinking this is all part of some game. Unaware of the danger they innocently giggle to each other, make grimaces and whisper into each other's ears as the *soldados* load their guns, not showing a shred of remorse for what they may be about to do.

Seeing that the *soldados* are both ready and waiting for their orders, the *Sinchi* turns towards them, and delivers the following commands in intervals of five or so seconds, '*Soldados* … load your weapons … Take aim … Ready … Fi …'

Before the *Sinchi* is able to pronounce his final command, one of the men Quispe had brought over when he interrupted the *Sinchi* for the second time steps in front of the firing squad and shouts, his words making a timely obstruction in the *Sinchi's* throat, '*Manam,*

manam! No shoot! *Sinchi*! Me know where *Senderistas* are! I talk! I take! Me! *Si*, me!'

This is such a shock that the *Sinchi*'s jaw locks shut. It takes him a few moments to loosen the mandible.

'Have they been here recently?'

Shaking his head, '*Manam, manam* now!'

'So they have been here recently?'

Shaking his head again, 'Now!'

'Oh, you mean now?'

'*Si*, now!'

'In light of your cooperation, I'll let you choose any four children you want to take out of the firing line. Four...'

Guided by one of the *soldados*, the young man chooses the four children he wants to remove from the firing line. The visual of this good-will gesture causes a group of four to five *comuneros* to step forward, calculating that if each took four, that ought to be enough to rescue the remaining children.

Standing side by side, the *comuneros* agree to step forward one by one, until the *Sinchi* allows them to retrieve the remaining children.

'I know where hide.'

'My son *Senderista*!'

'Base, know.'

'I show *Uma*.'

The *Sinchi* smiles for the first time, as if he means it, 'I want you all to know, in the utmost confidence, that whatever you've said here, will remain here. I…'

Stopping to catch his breath, the *Sinchi* loosens his throat by taking out his flask and having a swig of his beloved Pisco. How strange that his favourite drink is also the Quechua word for bird: *pisqo*. As he turns around to see the old man still unconscious, he takes another swig, but this time it's out of relief.

Debating whether or not to smoke his last cigarette, the *Sinchi* pauses to put his flask away. Is it time for the *Tumi* to come out and play? The *Sinchi* in him says not yet, as he steps back on the stone podium. Catching his breath, or trying to, all he can think about is getting this whole *comunero* business over with. So, he takes a last deep breath before readdressing his Andean audience, 'Fair enough. As promised, each of you is entitled to select any four children of your choice. Come on! Let's get on with things. I honestly don't have all…'

Before he can even finish his sentence, the four *comuneros* rush to pick four children apiece. The sound of laughter, as they innocently play around the wall, is all the praise they needed. However, the *Sinchi* knows too children would be left over, leaving him room for some high-stakes bargaining.

Glancing at the two remaining children, and then at the *comuneros*, the *Sinchi* has figured out exactly how to play this.

The *Sinchi* takes out his revolver, making sure everyone can see him loading in the missing bullets.

Once he is finished loading his gun, the *Sinchi* playfully spins the barrel a couple of times.

He finishes playing with the cylinder by snapping the gun shut with a flick of the wrist.

Then releasing the safety catch with a snap.

He's taking aim towards where the two remaining children are playing.

Now he pretends to make the motion of repetitive shooting.

Again he makes even louder shooting noises.

He looks at his gun.

He begins moving his neck in circles, as if trying to relax his muscles.

Seeing as there's no answer, he takes aim again.

The *Sinchi* fires a shot, purposely missing, inches away from one child's face.

Then takes aim at the other child.

The bullet ricochets off the stone wall and into the child, who falls to the ground. Women begin to wail. The rest of the children join in, holding on to their arms, shirt, whatever they can. The men, well, the men are reduced to nothingness because honestly, what could they do?

The wounded child is now lying in his mother's arms. Turns out – to the hidden relief of the *Sinchi* – that the bullet only scraped the side of one of the infant's legs. It is now bandaged by a colourful *chalina*. Its rainbow colours resemble the flag of *el Tahuantin-suyo*[27]. Pachamama had returned to pick up the dead and heal her wounded. However, no one claims the other child. He is standing quietly by the side of the wall.

Hearing no response, the *Sinchi* proceeds to raise the stakes once again.

He waits for about five seconds and then takes aim at the child.

Pulling the safety, 'One... Two... And...'

This time, he's nowhere close towards finishing his count when a woman, thirty-five years old, steps forward, revealing a *Senderista* bandana that was hidden under the neck of her sweater, 'I have fought for them on two occasions, sir.'

'Excuse me?'

'I said, I have fought for the *Senderistas* on two separate occasions, sir.'

She covers part of her face with the bandana, stands up straight and shouts, raising a fist up into the air, '*Viva la revolución! Viva el Presidente Gonzalo!*'

The *Sinchi* punches the woman in the stomach.

It takes her about two minutes to recover. In the mean time, the *Sinchi* plays with one of the pockets of his vest, trying to decide if he should have his last smoke. Maybe an accompanying drink. His little game as to what he should do is broken by the woman's reply; she's speaking in a weak yet coherent voice.

'They raped me and four other women. The others were either raped by more than one man at a time or killed alongside their husbands and children.'

'Throughout the whole thing I didn't make a sound. Not when they killed the children. Not when they beat my husband to death. They took me away with them because they saw me as being fit to join the cause. I spent over a year at one of their training schools...'

As if suffering from morning sickness, the woman gets on her hands and knees, vomiting into an imaginary toilet. The *comuner-*

os look elsewhere, as if trying to avoid eye contact, so she cannot see their looks of satisfaction. Maybe the *Sinchi* was a *Sinchi* in the classical sense of the word: ruthless, but just.

The *Sinchi* takes out his revolver and hits the woman across the head with the grip. In one quick motion, he removes the gun and its last forgotten bullet. The *Sinchi* shoots the woman in the chest, right around the heart.

For some inexplicable reason, he then grabs the woman and eases her to the ground. She is ready to return to Pachamama. The last thing she does is smile, as the *Sinchi* lays her down gently. He almost sheds a tear. The *Senderista* bandana she has tied around her neck slips upwards, covering her face like a veil of anonymity.

The *Sinchi* turns his focus towards the four *soldados* that gathered the children and shouts, '*Soldados*! Yes, you lot over there. Place her in the *Municipalidad* and burn it to the ground! Then, wait for further commands.'

The choir of *soldados* replies, 'Sir! Yes, sir!'

The *comuneros*' faces show a sea of mixed emotions. On the one hand, they are happy because the *Senderista* is dead and the children have been spared. On the other hand, they watch the *Municipalidad* go up into flames over the body of a person who did not even belong to this place. No one knows what to make of the day's proceedings because life in the *altiplano*[28] does not prepare you for these situations. Actually, it doesn't prepare you for anything at all.

By now, the *Sinchi* has grown detached from the world. Too much silence can sometimes toughen a man and after the day's events he's about as tough as *charqui*.

Watching the *Municipalidad* burn down, he knows he could never go back even if he wanted to. He no longer believes what he believed in before. Today he cremated the body of his remaining illusions. Education is a loaded gun. Love a bullet to the temple. Rank is what counts. The future holds only one possibility: to use his rank and education in order to spread his message throughout the region of Ayacucho. Methods would be subject to review.

With the job nearly finished and ciggie time approaching at death's corner, a few questions remain unanswered. What was she really doing out in the middle of nowhere? If she was a *Senderista*, why did she stand up for the *comuneros* whom she was meant to be watching? The more I think about things, the more I need and want magical realism to make sense of them.

After the *Municipalidad* has been burnt to a crisp, the wounded child attended to, and the old man regained consciousness, the events of the day begin to sink in. Some of the *comuneros* are perplexed, as to *how come a Sinchi was so loving to a Senderista?* Others are frightened to the point of hysteria. *Are they going to kill more of us? Will they burn us alive?* No one, not even the *soldados*, are sure of what to expect next.

As a result, some seek comfort in tears, while others are openly *chacchando* coca with their rotten, crooked, dark teeth. Though, I'd have to say that the most remarkable thing about the *comuneros* – despite what has happened – is their resilient silence, like that of the surrounding dormant mountains. Not one word!

The *soldados* are not manifesting their feelings so openly. Probably, they are thinking about the next *cholita* they are going to fuck for a fistful of coins. Even if they pay with a bank-note, the fact that both the money and the fuck would be worthless by the next morning pushes the men's sex drives into fifth gear. There's nothing quite like a fuck that you cannot be held accountable for. That is the ultimate rush of being a paramilitary: immunity!

Meanwhile, the *Sinchi* can be found sitting on his podium, searching for a pen and paper to jot down a sudden thought. It was inside one of the pages that he found a few 10,000 *Intis* notes and some tobacco scraps. What luck! Finally something is going his way. So, he stuffs the newly found contents into one of the empty side compartments of his Inner Tactical Vest for a later moment, making sure not to crumble the notes or wet the tobacco. The *Sinchi* is a da Vinci when it comes to the art of smoking.

Absurd, but the only conclusion the *Sinchi* can draw from his discovery, for he gives no sigh of relief or smile for his good fortune, is that now is as good a time as ever to smoke his final cigarette. In other words, he has found an excuse for justifying his vice to himself. '*It is medicinal*'. So he dips his dextrous, trusted left hand into the kitty and out comes the cigarette still smelling of this morning's innocence.

Taking out his *Tumi*-engraved lighter, the commanding *Sinchi* lights his ciggie. And I think we know which of the two he belongs to. What we don't know is why the *Sinchi* is smiling and laughing to himself.

His own laughter brings the *Sinchi* to a stop, since his breathing is partly obstructed. The *comuneros* and *soldados* have no idea what to make of his fit of hysterics. At least in previous attacks, his anger could be seen as a justifiable release, but this? It is a bit too much to take in.

At this stage the *Sinchi* couldn't care less what anyone else thinks. He tries to regain composure. But one glance at the blank looks of the *comuneros*' faces, like those of sheep, and he reverts to laughing like a madman.

It seems too much silence is not good for a man. More confused than ever, the *Sinchi* relights his cigarette. The *comuneros* just stand there, silently observing his every move. What a one-man pantomime this is! Perhaps the billowing smoke is trying to say something to him again? Perhaps not. Sometimes a cigarette is just a cigarette, although, as the *Sinchi* takes his final puff, some might disagree. For he stares deep into the billows of smoke that appear to suspend themselves before him. Only for him.

Half-warrior, half-shaman, he shows off his sorcery by extinguishing the cigarette on his left arm, as if he wishes to leave a permanent scar to remind him of the day's proceedings. Tattooed with indifference, the *Sinchi* decides to address the *comuneros* for the last time, as a farewell gesture. So, he takes his M16 assault rifle and fires a round into the air to gain everyone's attention. It works. The *comuneros* huddle in silence around the burning *Municipalidad*.

'*Comuneros*! Before I go, I want to thank you for your unrelenting cooperation during the last couple of hours. You are all a credit to rhetoric. Hard as it is for me to leave, I want you to know that a part of me will forever remain here, with you.'

At this point, the *comuneros*' silence seems like a vindictive act, or so the *Sinchi* interprets it. Their shunning silence is like that of the Amish towards those who have been excommunicated from the community. The feeling is a combination of shame and anger. That is exactly how the *Sinchi* feels.

To him, they all have the same dumb looks on their faces. Blank. Unintelligent. Ewe-like. And the *Sinchi* knows he is more of a butcher than a shepherd.

Fed up with trying to reason – or of attempting to make any type of fathomable exchange – with anyone or anything, the *Sinchi*'s rising blood pressure brings about another attack of tachycardia. He feels sweaty and feverish; his eyes become bloodshot.

He tries to regain his composure, but he can't. The last shred of the man of reason went up in flames with the *Municipalidad* today. Even if he wanted to explain things, what's the use? The only thing the *comuneros* seem to respond to, if anything, is fear. But don't we all? It's like asking a handful of people about what they want in life and expecting not to hear at least one of them say happiness or health.

The *Sinchi* looks at the *comuneros*, trying to sum things up. He pauses, reaches into one of the pockets of his Outer Tactical Vest with his left hand, removes a *Senderista* bandana, and ties it around his neck like a cowboy. Sometimes, visual aids are a useful tool of education, and his *soldados* follow suit. However, the *comuneros* reply to this symbolic gesture with even more taciturnity, as if they were internally praying to *Supay* not to harm them anymore with his devilish rage. After all, quiet is a synonym for peace.

The invocations are answered when for some inexplicable reason a confused *Sinchi* decides to put an end to his visit by addressing the *comuneros* with whatever words that feel like coming out.

'*Viva la guerra popular!*'

He exits the *Plaza de Armas* silently, as if he has just lost a major battle to an unknown superior force.

By the time we've caught up with him again, Mama Quillya has blessed us with the serenity of nightfall. Before we're returned to the darkness of creation, the last time we spot the *Sinchi*, he has become a black blur again. Like a shooting, fading star in the infinite night sky, he's somewhere — but where? Infinity knows nothing of place; neither does anger. All we know is that his voice, with each subsequent word, is growing less audible.

Hanan Pacha. Kay Pacha. Ukhu Pacha[29]. As if he were travelling between time, space, realities, the last words we are able to hear from the *Sinchi* are these instructions to Quispe, 'From now on, there will be no more of this shit. When we arrive at a village, the first thing we'll do is to gather all the *comuneros* — men, women, children, the elderly, the obese, the crippled, anyone who has a pulse – in their *Plaza de Armas*. Once there, we will ask the first one we pick out at random if they know anything about the *Senderistas*. If they say anything, we'll put the entire village in the buildings, pour kerosene all over, and set them on...'

The sounds of a few muffled, anonymous steps are the last things that can be heard. Or seen. Forget reflection. Forget religion. Forget everything because it's time to count the number of *desaparecidos*. Though, what I am unable to determine is if the smell of shit that has followed us throughout our journey today acts as a reminder of where we've been or are yet to go.

ENDNOTES

1 The guanaco and vicuña are South American camelids and relatives of the llama. The vicuña's fine, silky wool is especially valuable.

2 Inti was the Incan sun god. Mama Quillya was the moon and the wife of Inti. The inti was also a short-lived Peruvian currency in circulation between 1985-1991. It experienced a dramatic devaluation due to hyperinflation during the years of the Internal Conflict. The inti was itself a replacement for an inflation-stricken sol, and was replaced by the nuevo sol, still in circulation today.

3 Illapa was the Incan god of the weather. He was said to keep the Milky Way in a jug and use it to create rain. In Quechua, '*illapa*' means 'lightning'.

4 Pachamama was an Incan goddess and mother of Inti. Her name comes from the Quechuan words *pacha* (land) and *mama* (earth), and could be literally translated as 'mother earth'.

5 Mama Cocha was the Incan goddess of the sea.

6 Pacha Kamaq and Pariacaca were a pre-Incan creator god and goddess, associated with earth and water, respectively. The two were adopted into the Incan pantheon, albeit with lesser status.

7 *Los desaparecidos*, meaning 'the disappeared' was a phrase coined during the 70s in Argentina to refer to people kidnapped and executed without trial or record, or acknowledgement from the government. In the words of Argentinean general and coup leader Jorge Rafael Videla: 'The disappeared are just that: disappeared. They are neither alive nor dead. They are disappeared.'

8 *Chacchando* means grinding.

9 On the 26th of December, 1980, *Sendero Luminoso* hung dead dogs from lampposts in the centre of Lima with an inscription attached on to each dog denouncing Deng Xiaoping, leader of the People's Republic of China and successor to Chairman Mao, who was seen as having betrayed the revolutionary cause.

10 Names of the eleven provinces that form part of the Ayacucho region.

11 MRTA or el Movimiento Revolucionario Túpac Amaru was a Peruvian terrorist group, notorious for extortions, armed robberies, murders and kidnappings. The MRTA's name was homage to Túpac Amaru II, an 18th-century rebel leader himself named after his ancestor Túpac Amaru, the last indigenous monarch of the Neo-Inca State, a short-lived successor to the Incan Empire.

12 *Sendero Luminoso*, or 'Shining Path' is an extreme leftist terrorist organization that waged war on the Peruvian government from 1980 to 1993. *Sendero Luminoso* was responsible for over almost half of the 75,000 people either killed or disappeared in the period.

13 *MacGyver* was an 80s television show serialised by ABC. The show follows Angus MacGyver, an agent for a fictional US government agency. The episode formula involved MacGyver escaping life-threatening situations by crafting ingenious solutions out of everyday household items. The show led to the phrase 'MacGyverism', meaning an improvised solution to a problem that uses existing resources.

14 Spanish equivalent of 'better the devil you know'.

15 *Cordillera* means mountain range.

16 Uchuraccay is a village located in Huanta, Ayacucho. In 1983, seven journalists and their guide were killed by the townspeople, for reasons unknown.

17 *Comuneros* literally means 'member of the community', but is historically associated with anticolonial revolutionaries. In this story, it is used synonymously with *campesino*, meaning peasant or farmer.

18 The *Tren de las Sierras* is a regional rail line in Córdoba, and a historical locus for debate between privatisation and state ownership.

19 DNI: *Documento Nacional de Indentidad*. By law, every adult citizen of Peru is supposed to have an identity card.

20 *Trueque:* barter. Much of Peru operates on an informal economy of barter and exchange.

21 *Sinchi* is Quechua for warrior. During the period of the Peruvian Internal Conflict the government deployed the *Sinchis* (an American-funded counterterrorist brigade) to combat *Sendero Luminoso*. They were notorious for human rights violations.

22 Ayacucho is one of the 24 provinces that make up Peru. Its name derives from the Quechuan words *aya* (death) and *kuchu* (corner): death's corner. During the years of the Peruvian Internal Conflict, Ayacucho – the poorest area in the country at that time – experienced the worst of the violence. *Sendero Luminoso* made this province their headquarters, hoping to turn it into an exemplary model of a communist rural regime.

23 The highest quality silver used by Peruvian craftsmen in the 80s.

24 The *huayruro* (Ormosia coccinea) is a plant that produces red seeds, used for good luck charms and jewellery throughout Latin America.

25 *Cholo* is a derogatory term used to refer to people of indigenous heritage.

26 *Paco* is the Andean equivalent to a shaman.

27 *Tahuantinsuyo* was the Inca name for their empire. The rainbow Flag of Cusco is now associated with the name, though the Inca Empire never had an official flag.

28 The *altiplano* is the Andean Plateau, an area of high plateau that spans Bolivia, Peru, Argentina, and Chile.

29 The three *Pachas* are the three worlds into which the Incas divided the cosmos. *Hanan Pacha* refers to the world above, *Kay Pacha* to this world, and *Ukhu Pacha* to the underworld.

Deep thanks to
Oliver Jones, who worked closely with
me to improve this text and iron out infelicities. His
notes are also expert and informative. A special nod
to Alexandra Payne for her excellent editing also. Professor
Sheila Hillier for her early editorial notes and suggestions of
an earlier draft. Finally, a tip of the hat to designer
Edwin Smet, and Dr Swift, who believed
in this story.